First published in Japan in 1986 by Shiko-Sha Co., Ltd., Tokyo,
under the title *Yuudachino Tomodachi*.
Published in the United States, Great Britain, Canada, Australia, and New Zealand in 2010
by North-South Books Inc., an imprint of NordSüd Verlag AG, CH-8005 Zürich, Switzerland.
Distributed in the United States by North-South Books Inc., New York 10001.
Library of Congress Cataloging-in-Publication Data is available.
ISBN: 978-0-7358-2285-6 (trade edition).
Printed in China by SNP Leefung Packaging & Printing (Dongguan) Co., Ltd., Dongguan, P.R.C., October 2009
1  3  5  7  9 • 10  8  6  4  2
www.northsouth.com

Kazuo Iwamura

# HOORAY for SUMMER!

NorthSouth
New York / London

One summer afternoon, Mick, Mack, and Molly were playing in the field.

"It's too hot," croaked a tired frog in a patch of shade. Even the grass and the flowers in the field did not move. Everything was still. Everything, that is, but the little squirrel children. Mick, Mack, and Molly were hopping around as usual.

Suddenly a flock of birds was flying away. "Go home, little squirrels!" one cried. "The rain will start soon!"

"Wonderful!" croaked the frog. "It will be nice and cool then."

"Oh, no! We'd better go home," Mick told his brother and sister. "Let's run back to the woods."

But before they had even reached the trees, it started to rain.

*PLIP! PLOP! PLIP! PLOP!* Down came the big drops.

*SWIIIIISHHHH.* Grasses stirred in the rain.

"Hurry!" said Mick. They ran as fast as they could.

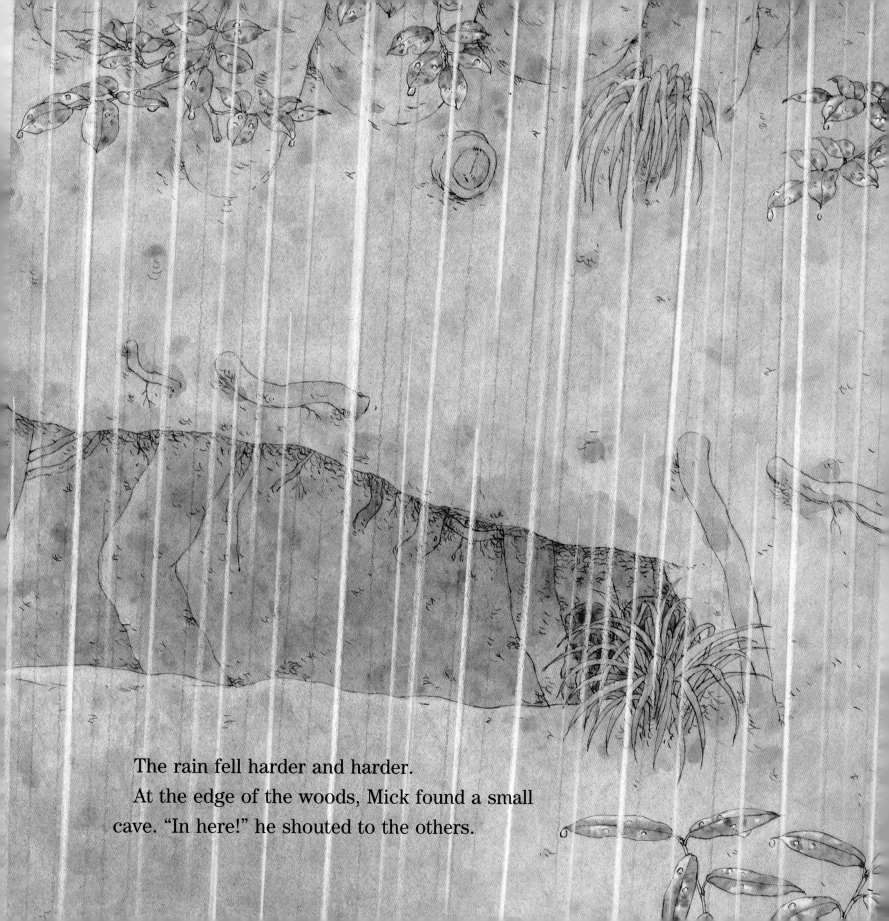

The rain fell harder and harder.
At the edge of the woods, Mick found a small
cave. "In here!" he shouted to the others.

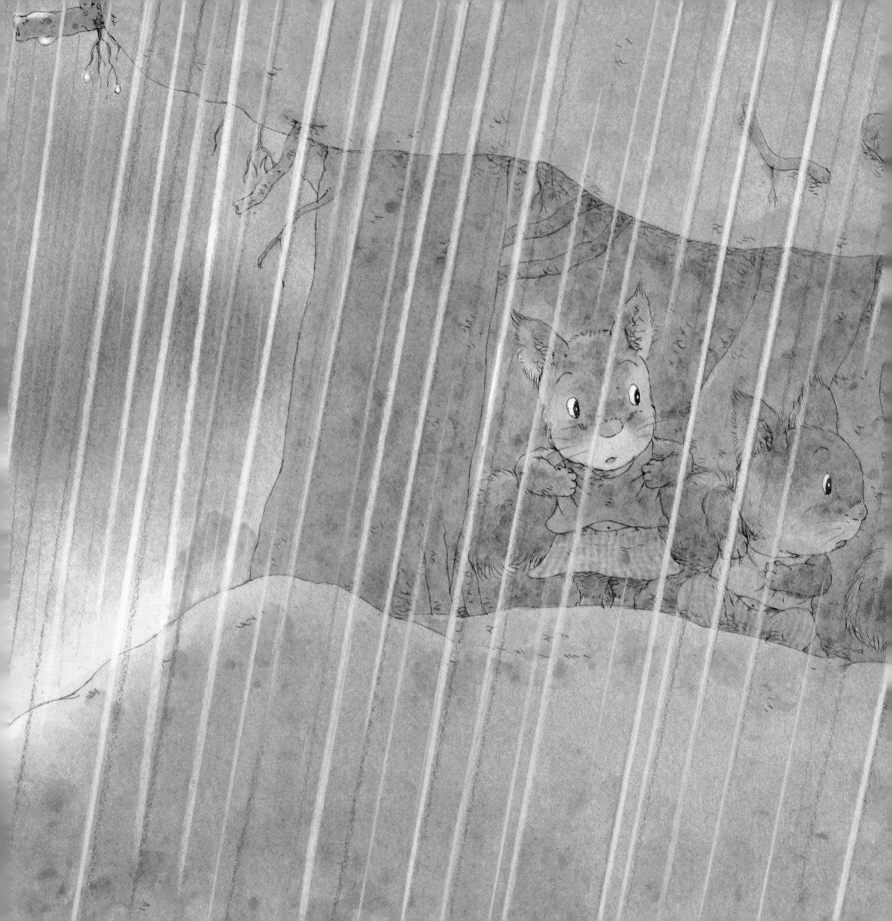

"Oh!" said Mick. "There's someone here already."
At the end of the cave sat two little mice, a brother
and a sister.
"Are you hiding from the rain here too?" Mick asked.
"Yes," said the mouse boy timidly.

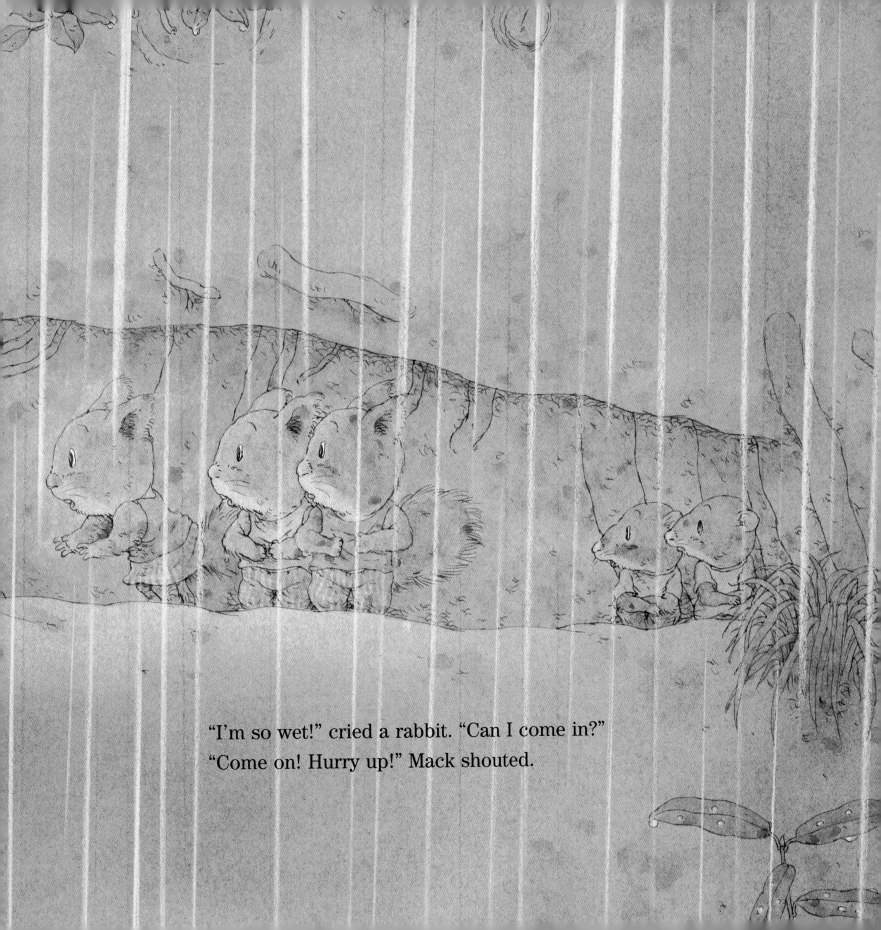

"I'm so wet!" cried a rabbit. "Can I come in?"
"Come on! Hurry up!" Mack shouted.

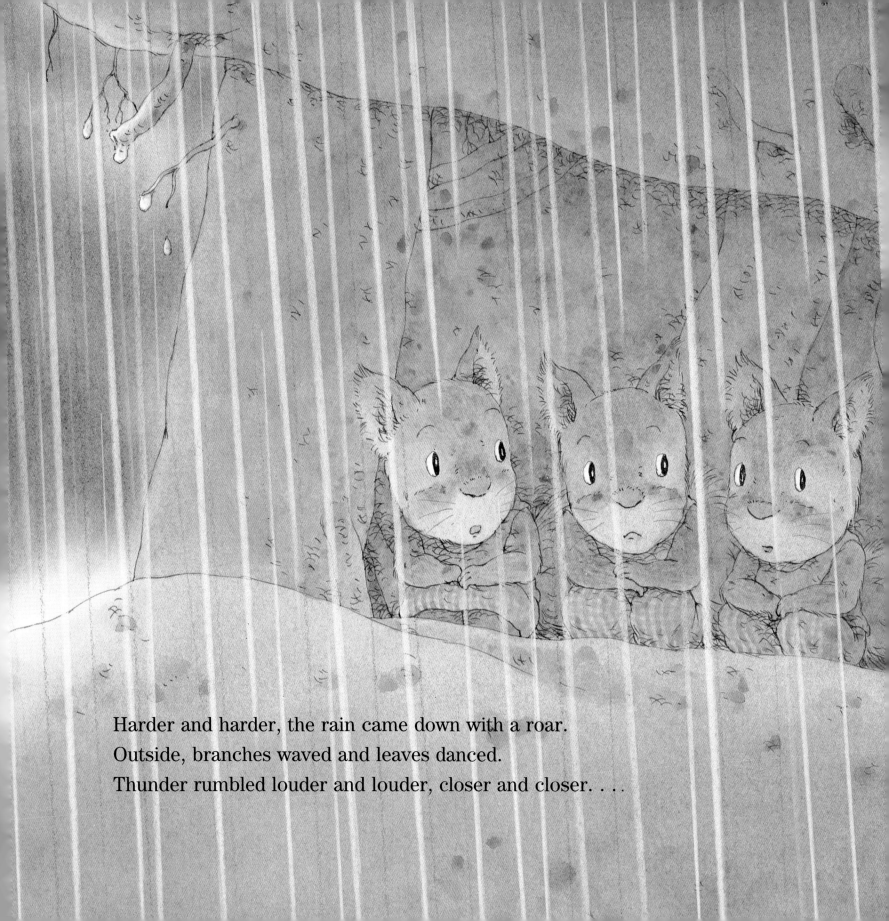

Harder and harder, the rain came down with a roar.
Outside, branches waved and leaves danced.
Thunder rumbled louder and louder, closer and closer. . . .

CRACK! BOOM!
Lightning flashed right outside the cave.
"Oh, no!"
"Help!"

Everyone trembled with fear. "Mommy!" The little mouse girl gave a little shriek.

At last the rain stopped. The sky grew brighter.
"The storm is over!" said Molly.
Outside the cave, rain dripped off the trees and grasses. A tear dripped from the little mouse girl's eye too.

"Let's go play on the seesaw together!" Mick shouted. There was a cool breeze in the field now. Raindrops sparkled on the flowers. All sorts of little animals came out from hiding. The earth smelled clean.

"We are the Summer Storm Friends!" said Mick.

"Hooray for new friends!" shouted Mack.

"Hooray for summer storms!" shouted Molly.

"Hooray for summer!" shouted everyone.

And they all played together in the field until the cicadas told them it was time to go home for supper.

WITHDRAWN